To Alexis, who created the ORIGINAL Pipsie. To Matt, who is the INSPIRATION behind everything Alfred. And to Nancy, who is NANCY . . . a true ORIGINAL and my INSPIRATION.
—R.D.

For Mela, Laura, Renée, Christina, and Joy.
Thank you for always cheering me on.
—T.B.

Acknowledgments:
The MAGIC of Pipsie: the support of Debbie, Rafe, Amy, Tom, and so many others; the uddergenius of Dave; the spirit of PVHS Hornets Class of '73; a real-life girl named Pipsie from New Orleans; Ms. P. a third-grade teacher who drew Pipsie posters to welcome us to her class. Thank you all for this AMAZING adventure.
—R.D.

A LURIE INK Book

Text copyright © 2016 by Rick DeDonato
Illustrations copyright © 2016 by Tracy Bishop

Published by Two Lions, New York
www.apub.com

Amazon, the Amazon logo, and Two Lions are trademarks of Amazon.com, Inc., or its affiliates.

ISBN-13: 978-1-5039-5061-0 (hardcover)
ISBN-10: 1-5039-5061-1 (hardcover)
ISBN-13: 978-1-5039-5053-5 (paperback)
ISBN-10: 1-5039-5053-0 (paperback)

Book design by Tanya Ross-Hughes

Printed in China

First Edition

10 9 8 7 6 5 4 3 2 1

PIPSIE,
nature detective

THE LUNCHNAPPER

Written by Rick DeDonato
Illustrated by Tracy Bishop

two lions

It was a WONDERFUL day for a school trip.

"This is going to be the BEST school trip ever!"
Pipsie told her friend Alfred Z. Turtle.
"Hurry—we're going on a nature scavenger
hunt in the woods."

Alfred hurried s—l—o—w—l—y because
that's how turtles hurry.

Can't forget our
peanut butter and
jelly sandwiches!

LUNCH

Pipsie loved scavenger hunts.
Especially nature scavenger hunts.

After all, she was a nature detective.

Pipsie and Alfred arrived just in time.

"Welcome, nature EXPLORERS!" Ranger Nancy said.
"Are you ready for a real adventure?"

"Y-e-e-e-e-s!" Everyone cheered.

"Great!" she said. "Pick a nature BUDDY, and
let's get started."

Pipsie picked Alfred, naturally!

Pipsie's twin friends, Lexi and Max, picked each other.

Pipsie's next-door neighbor Buckey picked Dewey.

"Here's a list of Seven Wonders of Nature," said Ranger Nancy. "If you find all seven, you'll win a prize!"

She gave each team a camera. "Every time you see something on the list, take a picture."

SEVEN WONDERS of NATURE!

#1 AN ANIMAL'S HOME
#2 ANIMAL TRACKS
#3 A SIGN THAT AN ANIMAL WAS HERE!
#4 SOMETHING CRAWLING
#5 SOMETHING FLYING
#6 SOMETHING SWIMMING
#7 YOUR FAVORITE WONDER

"Your buddy is a TURTLE? Ha-ha." Dewey laughed.
"Turtles are too slow. A turtle is a terrible partner."

Pipsie scowled. Sometimes Dewey could be rude.
"Alfred is the PERFECT partner.
He's CLEVER and FUN, and he knows all about nature.
Plus, he rides a scooter better than anyone I know!"

"Nature Scavenger Hunters, when you hear this whistle, the hunt is over," Ranger Nancy said. "Ready, set, get going!"

"Come on, Alfred! It's time to find our Seven Wonders of Nature," Pipsie said.

Pipsie started for the woods—and stopped.
"Alfred, where's our lunch? It was here just a
minute ago. And now it's GONE."

Looks like we have a lunchnapper!

"Looks like we have a nature hunt
AND a mystery to solve!" Pipsie said.
"What could be better than that?"

Groovy,
but not lunch.

Alfred looked DOWN on the ground.
He saw SOMETHING CRAWLING.

"SOMETHING CRAWLING!
That's EXCELLENT!" said Pipsie.
"That's #4 on our list."

Pipsie looked UP to the treetop.

"Look, Alfred . . . a bird's-nest hole.
We found #1 on the list, too—
an ANIMAL'S HOME!"

Nice, but still not lunch.

"Tap, tap, tap." Pipsie and Alfred heard a noise.

"Alfred, that's a CLUE," Pipsie said. "That tapping tells us what kind of bird made the nest."

"And there he is!" Pipsie said.
"A woodpecker—SOMETHING FLYING!
Wowee! We found three things already!"

G-r-u-m-b-l-e r-u-m-b-l-e.

"What's THAT noise?" Pipsie asked.

That's a clue that someone needs to eat!

It was Alfred's stomach! He was getting hungry.

Pipsie was getting hungry, too. "Let's go back to that rock and look for clues to find our lunch!" she said.

Pipsie and Alfred searched HIGH and LOW and ROUND and ROUND.

Suddenly, Pipsie heard Alfred cry out.

O-w-w-i-e Z-o-w-w-i-e!

Oh, no! Something was stuck in Alfred's foot.

"Let me *see*—that could be a clue!" Pipsie said.

It was a porcupine QUILL.

Was the porcupine the lunch thief?

"Hmm, porcupines are nocturnal. That means they only come out at night," Pipsie said. "So no thief, but you found A SIGN THAT AN ANIMAL WAS HERE!"

Alfred pointed to footprints
on the ground.

He thought they were Dewey's.

Was Dewey the lunch thief?

"Those aren't Dewey's footprints," Pipsie told Alfred. "Those are deer tracks . . .

. . . and there are the deer."

"We just found #2 on the list—ANIMAL TRACKS!" Pipsie said.

They walked deeper into the woods,
looking for lunch clues.

Before long, they saw Buckey and Dewey . . .
with a lunch bag that looked just like theirs!

There are
the lunchnappers!

Dewey reached into the
bag and took out . . .

. . . a hot dog.

Nope. Not their lunch.

Ewww! COLD hot dogs!

"Over there!" Pipsie shouted. "More animal tracks!"

"It looks like the animal was dragging something. Maybe it's our lunch! Let's make this mystery history!"

They followed the tracks toward the sound of a g-u-r-g-l-i-n-g stream.

"Beavers!" Pipsie said. "I don't think they stole our lunch. Beavers mostly eat trees and plants! And they weren't dragging our lunch. Those are the marks their big flat tails make when they walk!"

Pipsie and Alfred still hadn't found their lunch, but they had found #6— SOMETHING SWIMMING!

"Good news, Alfred! We just need a picture of #7—
our FAVORITE WONDER—and then we'll have
everything on the list."

But Alfred looked sad. Even his shell drooped a little.
Their lunch was still missing.

"Don't give up, Alfred. Without a doubt, we'll figure this out!"

Pipsie opened her detective notebook and wrote down the FACTS.

FACTS
☑ The porcupine didn't take our lunch.
☑ The deer didn't take our lunch.
☑ The beaver didn't take our lunch. And there are no more footprints to follow.

I wish I had wings.

Alfred flapped his arms.

He wished he could fly.

Then he'd be able to look down and see who took their lunch.

Pipsie jumped up.

"Alfred, that's it! You just gave me a BIG clue.
I have a hunch who took our lunch! And I know
how to prove it!"

Pipsie looked at their pictures carefully.
"Yes! I'm right! The lunch thief is . . ."

Ranger Nancy blew her whistle. The scavenger
hunt was over.

And they didn't have a picture of their
FAVORITE WONDER.

Alfred's shell had a terrible case of the droopies now.

"Don't worry, Alfred," Pipsie said. "We DO have
everything we need! You'll see. . . ."

Everyone gathered around Ranger Nancy.

Dewey and Buckey didn't have SOMETHING SWIMMING.
But Lexi and Max had pictures of everything!

"We have everything, too," Pipsie chimed in.

"A bird's NEST. Deer TRACKS. A porcupine QUILL.

A worm CRAWLING. A woodpecker FLYING.
Beavers SWIMMING."

Pipsie smiled. "And here's a picture of our Favorite
Wonder of Nature . . . with the thief who took our lunch!"

"Our Favorite Wonder of Nature is Alfred," Pipsie said.
"And there's the lunch thief behind him! A crow!"

Our lunch
flew away!

"Good work, Pipsie!" Ranger Nancy said. "But Alfred can't
be your Favorite Wonder because he was on your team.
The winners are Lexi and Max."

"It's okay, Alfred," said Pipsie. "This was still the BEST school trip ever. We solved the mystery—and you're still MY Favorite Wonder of Nature! Case closed. Now, let's find something to eat!"

FUN FACTS

EARTHWORMS do not have lungs. They breathe through their skin!

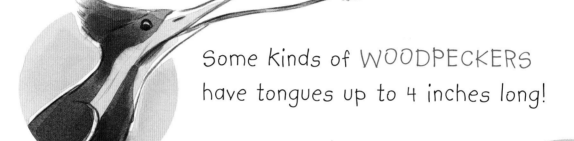

Some kinds of WOODPECKERS have tongues up to 4 inches long!

The PORCUPINE has thousands of quills on its back that protect it from enemies!

Baby porcupines are called "porcupettes."

Most DEER are herbivorous, which means they eat only plants.

BEAVERS build dome-like homes, called lodges, using branches and mud. And they can be reached only by underwater entrances!

Beavers use their tails to warn other beavers of danger by slapping their tails against the water.

CROWS are very intelligent. Sometimes they work together to steal food from other animals. And they can use and make tools. They have been seen shaping sticks to poke into holes looking for food!

Crows can imitate a human voice!

WOODLAND TRACKS

Beaver

Front Foot

Hind Foot

Porcupine

Front Foot

Hind Foot

Dewey!

Deer

Bird

Rabbit

Wildlife insight by Jason Davis, wildlife biologist